For Peter Natti and
for Gretel, Barnaby and Talbot Porter

PETER'S LONG WALK

by Lee Kingman Pictures by Barbara Cooney

Doubleday & Company, Inc., Garden City, New York

9

Peter lived in the country.

Peter had a cat who dashed about when he threw a ball to her.

4

Peter had a dog who splashed about when he threw sticks in the pond for him.

Peter had sheep who pattered up when he threw bread to them.

Peter had ducks who chattered up when he threw corn to them.

But Peter's house was away off by itself in the woods, and there wasn't another boy or girl who lived near enough to play with Peter.

Peter was as lonely as a chicken in an egg.

"You just wait," said Peter's mother. "When you are five years old and go to school in the village, you'll have someone to play with every day."

So Peter waited. He waited all the long, long year he was four. Finally, on a bright spring day, Peter grew up and was five!

But before he blew out the candles on his birthday cake, Peter thought a wish — the wish he always wished. "I wish I could find someone to play with me."

Peter looked at the five candles winking at him. Then he shut his eyes tight and blew, for if all the candles went out, his wish would come true.

But when he opened his eyes, he saw one candle still blinking at him!
He must have blown right around a corner and missed it.

"Now my wish won't come true!" he cried.

Peter felt as lonely as an island in the sea.

"That just means it won't come true all by itself," Peter's mother said.
"You'll have to make it come true by yourself instead."

So then and there Peter made up his mind! His mother had said when he was five years old and went to school in the village he would have someone to play with him. So tomorrow he would go to the village and make his wish come true all by himself!

Early the next morning, before his mother was even awake, Peter ran out of the farmyard gate. He was off to the village to go to school. He had forgotten that his mother said it was a very long walk!

For a while Peter trotted joyfully, but it was a long walk. Before long he sat down on a rock to rest.

Suddenly he knew someone was watching him. Perhaps it was someone who would play with him.

He turned around and looked around, but he couldn't see anything. He felt a scared little shiver run down his back and up his back.

There was Peter, all by himself on a long walk, and he felt as lonely as a turtle in his shell.

But Peter was on his way to school at last. So he jumped up and trudged hopefully. It was a long walk. After a while he sat down by a brook to rest. Suddenly he knew someone was watching him. Perhaps it was someone who would play with him.

He turned around and looked around, but he couldn't see anything. He felt a frightened little quiver run down his back and up his back.

There was Peter, all by himself on a long walk, and he was as lonely as a dog without a tail.

But Peter was on his way to school at last. So he jumped up and walked bravely. It was a very long walk. After a while he sat down under a tree to rest.

Suddenly he knew someone was watching him. Perhaps it was someone who would play with him.

He turned around and looked around, but he couldn't see anything. He felt a very big scare, just sticking in his throat.

There was Peter all by himself on such a long walk to the village, and he felt as lonely as the sun in the sky.

But Peter was on his way to school at last, and even though he was hot and tired, he went slowly on down the road.

Finally he came out of the tangled trees at the edge of the woods. There was a house and another house. Then there were lots of houses, and Peter knew he had come to the village.

Now he would find someone to play with him!

Peter looked all around at the neat little houses tucked into their flower

beds. He saw cars driving along and trucks driving along. He saw people running to get on a bus. He saw a milkman and a mailman. But he didn't see any boys and girls anywhere! Perhaps they were already inside the school.

Then Peter stood still right in the middle of the village. How would he know which building was the school? He thought he would find it when he saw all the boys and girls playing outside.

Suddenly a lady running for a bus nearly tripped over Peter. "My goodness!" she said. "Are you growing there on the sidewalk?"

"No," said Peter. "I'm looking for the school."

"Well, you're looking right at it," the lady said rather crossly.

So Peter didn't tell her he wasn't sure what a school looked like. He crossed the street and walked into the big yard.

There was the school, so white in the morning sunshine it seemed to sparkle! Peter felt as if there were sparkles running around inside him, too.

Here he was at school! Now surely he would find someone to play with him.

But all he saw was an old man sweeping the steps. Peter ran to him. "Where are all the boys and girls?"

"You're early," the man said.

"No one has come to play yet?" Peter asked.

"No. You must be new. I haven't seen you before."

"No," said Peter proudly. "Today is the first day I've ever come to school. I was five just yesterday."

"Oh, dear!" said the man, and he sat down on the steps beside Peter. "You're five and all grown up and you can't wait to come to school. That's just a shame, because you look so eager. But I'm afraid they won't let you come."

"Why?" Peter asked.

"It's a rule," said the man. "Everyone has to start school in September, all at the same time — like starting a race. You see, now you're five, well, that's really something! But you'll have to wait until next September and start school the same time as all the other boys and girls who are five. So now you just better run home quick."

Peter was a very brave boy.

Peter didn't cry.

But all his life he'd waited to go to school, and now he had to go home
— without anyone to play with him. Very slowly he started on the long
walk home.

Peter felt as lonely as a cloud going nowhere.

By the time poor Peter had trudged through the village and back up the long road into the woods, he was so tired he could hardly lift up his feet.

When he came to the big tree where he had rested that morning, he sat down again. He forgot it was the very place where he felt someone was watching him.

Suddenly a little surprise ran down his back and up his back. Someone was watching him!

There was a fat little rabbit looking at Peter.

"Hello!" cried Peter. "Would you play with me?"

The rabbit wiggled his ears and twitched his nose and bobbed his head. When Peter started up the road, the rabbit ran along with him for a little way.

"I guess I've found someone to play with after all," said Peter. He felt as happy as a grin.

But suddenly the rabbit jumped into the bushes and out of sight!
Poor Peter. He didn't have anyone to play with after all.

When he came to the brook where he had rested that morning, he sat down again. He forgot it was the very place where he felt someone was watching him!

Suddenly a surprise ran up his back and down his back. Someone was watching him!

There was a gay raccoon looking at Peter.

"Hello!" cried Peter. "Would you play with me?"

The raccoon looked at him as if he were quite shy, and went back to washing his lunch in the brook. It made Peter hungry to see him eat. So

he started up the road again, but the raccoon came and walked along with him a little way.

"I guess I've found someone to play with after all," said Peter. He felt as joyful as a dance.

But suddenly the raccoon swished his tail and jumped into the bushes and out of sight.

Poor Peter! He didn't have anyone to play with after all.

When he came to the rock he had rested on that morning, he sat down again. He forgot it was the very place where he felt someone was watching him!

Suddenly a surprise ran up his back and down his back — and up again. Someone was watching him!

There was a little gray fox looking at Peter.

"Hello!" cried Peter. "Would you play with me?"

The fox grinned and waved his tail, and when Peter started up the road, the fox walked along with him a little way.

"I guess I've found someone to play with me after all," said Peter. He felt as gay as a whistle.

But suddenly the fox jumped into the bushes and out of sight. There was Peter, all alone again on his long walk, and lonelier than he had ever been before.

It was just too much! Peter was so cross and tired he stamped along the
road and kicked stones. But before he knew it, there was the gate to his
house. And what do you suppose he saw waiting for him?

His cat and his dog and his sheep and his ducks were all at the gate,
just waiting for Peter to come home and play with them!

The cat was just waiting for Peter to throw the ball she had in her mouth.

The dog was just waiting for Peter to throw the stick he had in his mouth.

The sheep were just waiting for Peter so they could play tag with him.

The ducks were just waiting for Peter so they could dance with him.

Peter hurried into the yard. He threw sticks for his dog and the ball for his cat. He played tag with the sheep, and he danced with the ducks. Why, he had friends after all, and they all wanted to play with him!

And Peter wasn't sure, but he thought when he looked quickly behind him that he saw a rabbit scuttle behind a stone, and a fox rustle into the bushes, and a raccoon run down the path toward the pond!

"Peter!" called his mother. "I've been calling and calling you for breakfast. Where have you been?"

"I went for a long walk," said Peter, "and all by myself I found a lot of friends to play with me."

And do you know, Peter didn't tell his mother that he had gone to school. That's Peter's secret — and yours.